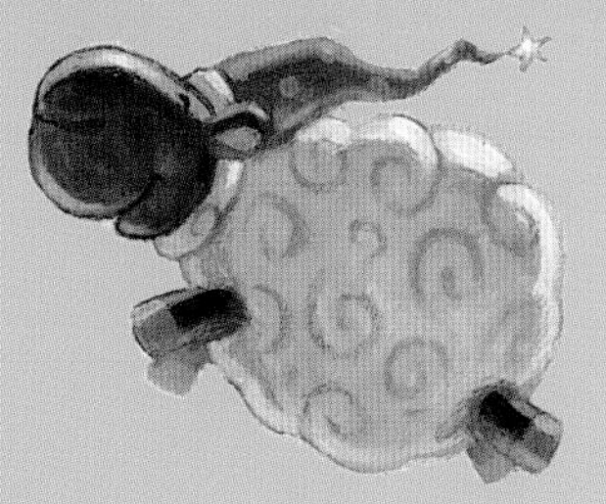

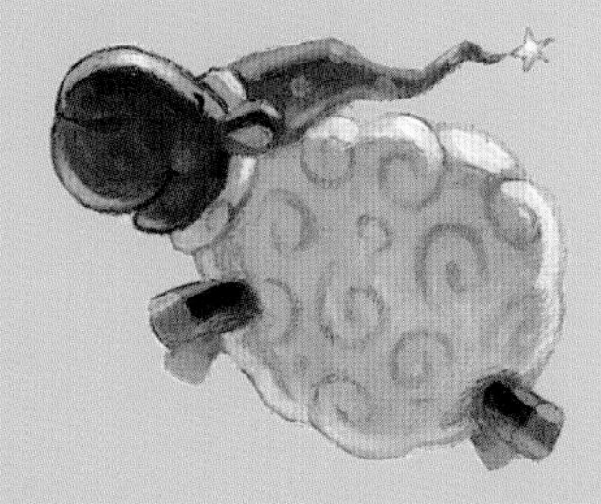

Susanna Leonard Hill illustrated by **Mike Wohnoutka**

Walker & Company New York

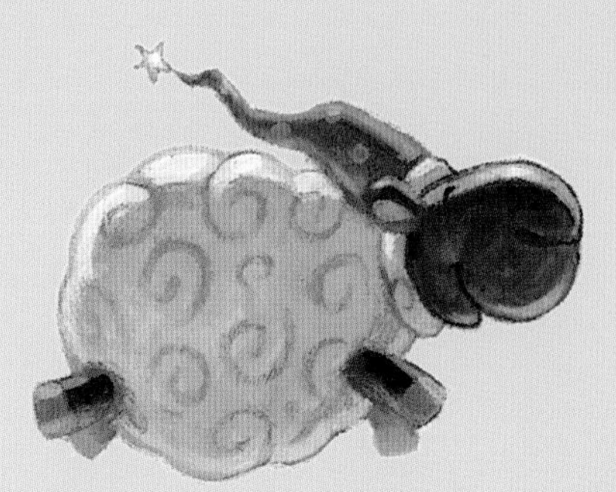

First published in the United States of America in September 2010
by Walker Publishing Company, Inc., a division of Bloomsbury Publishing, Inc.
www.bloomsburykids.com

For information about permission to reproduce selections from this book, write to
Permissions, Walker BFYR, 175 Fifth Avenue, New York, New York 10010

Library of Congress Cataloging-in-Publication Data
Hill, Susanna Leonard.
Can't sleep without sheep / Susanna Leonard Hill ; illustrated by Mike Wohnoutka.
p. cm.
Summary: When counting sheep does not help Ava fall asleep and the sheep complain that they are exhausted, they send in replacements, including cows, horses, penguins, and pigs, but none prove satisfactory.
ISBN 978-0-8027-2066-5 (hardcover) • ISBN 978-0-8027-2067-2 (reinforced)
[1. Sheep—Fiction. 2. Animals—Fiction. 3. Sleep—Fiction.]
I. Wohnoutka, Mike, ill. II. Title. III. Title: Cannot sleep without sheep.
PZ7.H55743Can 2010 [E]—dc22 2009054215

Art created with acrylic paint
Typeset in Bernhard Gothic Medium
Book design by Donna Mark

Printed in China by Hung Hing Printing (China) Co., Ltd., Shenzhen, Guangdong
1 3 5 7 9 10 8 6 4 2 (hardcover)
1 3 5 7 9 10 8 6 4 2 (reinforced)

All papers used by Bloomsbury Publishing, Inc., are natural, recyclable products made from wood grown in well-managed forests. The manufacturing processes conform to the environmental regulations of the country of origin.

For Eric, with love
—S. L. H.

To Franklin and Olivia, sweet dreams
—M. W.

Ava had a hard time falling asleep.
Her mind was always so busy!

"Try counting sheep," suggested her mother.
So she did.

"One sheep jumping over the fence . . . two sheep jumping over the fence . . . three sheep jumping over the fence . . ."

But her mind was full of ideas and questions, thoughts of today, and plans for tomorrow.

Night after night, the sheep had to jump the fence *many* times.

"Can we *please* stop?" asked the sheep. "We're exhausted."

"No! I need you to keep jumping!" said Ava.

"In that case," said the sheep, "we quit."

"You can't quit!" said Ava. "How will I get to sleep?"

"Don't worry. We'll find a replacement," they promised.

Horses seemed like the best choice. But they were so beautiful that Ava made the fence higher and wider to see how well they could jump.

"Horses are too much fun!" said the sheep. "We need somebody less pretty. Send in the chickens."

The chickens *tried* to get over the fence.

They *wanted* to get over the fence.

Ava laughed and laughed, but she did not go to sleep.

"We need somebody less ridiculous," said the sheep. "Pigs?"

The pigs were not in any hurry.

"One pig over the fence," said Ava. Then she had to wait while the others stopped to snack.

"Pigs are too slow," decided the sheep.

The cows were a complete disaster!

This was harder than the sheep thought!
But they were just getting started.

The penguins looked at the fence, then looked at themselves.

"We need a plan," they said.

"Next!" said the sheep.

The hippos waddled forward.
"This could take a while," said one sheep.

The animals grew impatient.

"Is it our turn?" asked the herd of buffalo.

"No, *we're* next!" shouted the flamingos, the armadillos, and the beavers.

"We'll see about that!" roared the buffalo.

The stampede began as the buffalo charged the fence.

Dust rose in clouds. Splinters flew everywhere. It was chaos!

“STOP!” cried Ava. “I’ll never get to sleep like this!”

"Wow," said the sheep. "Who knew we'd be so hard to replace?"
"I knew," Ava replied. "You always show up for work. You line up nicely and jump calmly. You're fluffy and peaceful and perfect!"

"Well," said one sheep. "It's nice to be appreciated."

"Please, will you stay?" begged Ava. "I need you to help me fall asleep."

"Don't worry," said the sheep. "You can count on us!"

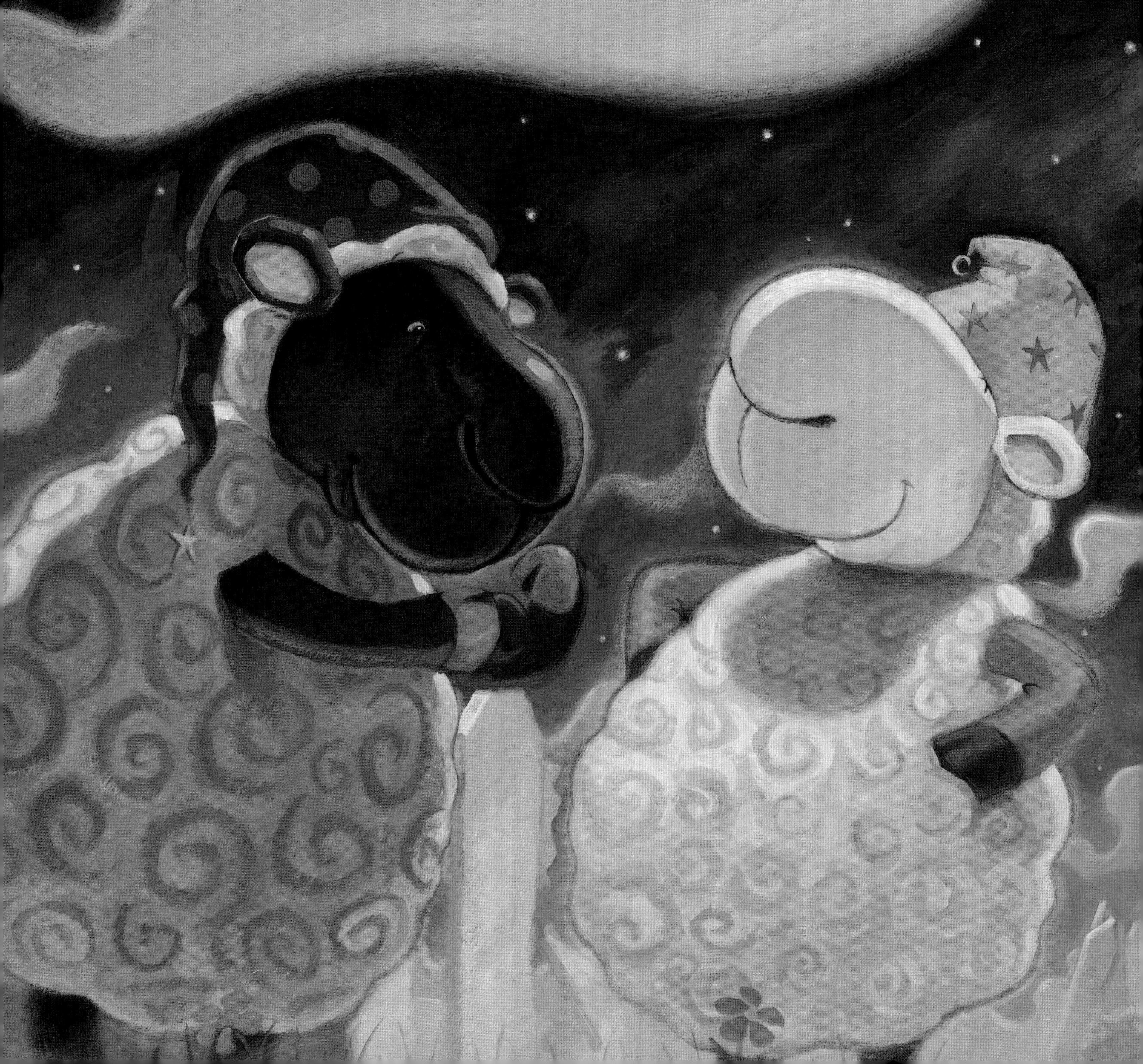

So she did.